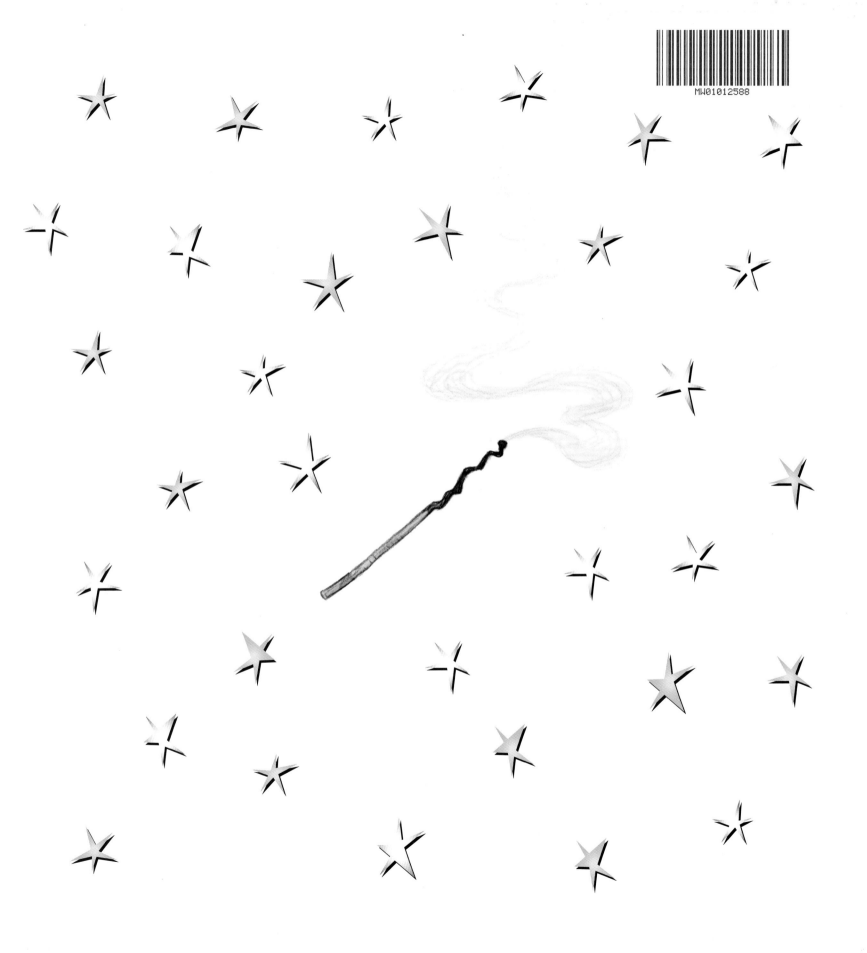

MW01012588

GONE WITH THE

WAND

a fairy's tale

by MARGIE PALATINI

pictures by
BRIAN AJHAR

ORCHARD BOOKS

AN IMPRINT OF
SCHOLASTIC INC.
NEW YORK

Once upon a time. Long, long ago...

(To be actual and completely factual, this little fairy's tale
began three months ago last Thursday.)

If yours truly, Tooth Fairy Second Class, Edith B. Cuspid,
hadn't seen it with my own two peepers, I wouldn't have
believed it myself.

But — there she was, all right.

Yes, my dears. Bernice Sparklestein, once the best
Fairy Godmother in the entire universe and beyond,
was having a bad wand day.

A very bad wand day.

She wasn't even having luck stirring up a little tea for two.

"Perhaps you dipped when you should have dunked?" I suggested.

"I'm **kapoofski** is what I am!" cried Bernice. "Edith, I think my wand is — gone."

I almost choked on my crumpet.

What? Bernice Sparklestein,
gone with the wand?
Rubbish!

Why, her work was legendary! The stuff stories were made of.
And she had the pictures to prove it!

Gone with the wand? Utter nonsense.
I told Bernice to just get out there and
give that wand another whirl.
Shoulders back.
Feet forward.
The big windup.

Yes, well . . .

Perhaps she was even rustier than we both imagined.

Frankly, it looked like she didn't even have enough
bippidy left in her to salacadoo one more pumpkin.

Yes, those glory, fire-breathing dragon days
were over, all right.

"I should have gone into your line of work, Edith. Tooth fairies are always busy."

"I know everyone believes the nightlife is glamorous, but, all that tippy-toeing is not easy on the feet, I can tell you. Look at this bunion."

Bernice winced at my big toe.

"Oh me, oh my! I don't think I could handle that sort of work, Edith. What ever am I going to do now?"

A very good question.

Of course, barely passing my wisdom tooth test myself,
it was not one I was able to answer on such short notice.

But, then, don't you know, suddenly a decidedly *divine* idea
popped into the old cranium.

I never breathed a word of it before, but oh my, yes,
I had my share of fairied experience before I landed
in the tooth business. Dozens and dozens, well, just eons of
doing this or that.

My closets and trunks were filled with old uniforms
and folderol.

Maybe Bernice could try them on for size and
see if any fit her fantasy.

We winged it right on over to my place.

"Fairy Dusting. Positively *charming*! You know, Bernice, everyone can use a little magic sprinkle now and then."

Bernice tied on the apron and headed up, up, and away.

She was back in ten minutes.

"I tink I'mb allergic to dust!
Aaaa — Aaaa — Aaaa . . ."

I handed her a hankie and we went back to the closet.

"Chooooooooo!"

"Now, here is a simply spectacular sparkler," I said, pulling out another little number from the closet. "Snow Fairy! Creating snowflakes is *so* creative, my dear."

"Fancy schmancy, too," agreed Bernice, getting ready for takeoff number two.

She was back in ten minutes.

"B-B-B-Brrrrr. My w-w-w-wings iced up over B-B-B-Buffalo."
We brushed off the flakes and went back to the closet.

"Aha! This sugarplum look is totally
marvelous," I said. "Besides, nobody can resist
a candygram! I can tell you from experience,
everyone's got a sweet tooth!
"So, ta-ta and tootle-loo!"

Bernice headed out and up.

She was back in five hours and ten minutes.

"I ate the merchandise," she confessed,
bursting out of her sugarplums.

(*My dears, it was not pretty.*)

"I'm a failure!" Bernice said tearfully.

"Oh, pooh!" I said with a hug. "So you're not a duster,
flaker, or big with the bonbons. Don't you worry.
We'll find a job that's perfect for you yet."

Bernice wiped a tear. "Really?"

"But of course!"

I fibbed.

Truthfully, what does a Fairy
Godmother do when her wand is
really gone?

. . . Who gives a wish to
a wishmaker?

Granted, I was only a plain old ordinary pillow tooth plucker, but I knew I had to think of something to help my best friend. And fast.

So, I thought and pondered.

Pondered and thought.

And then I just pondered, pondered, pondered.

I pondered so much I was pooped.

Before I knew it, I nodded off for forty winks myself.

And then — Aha!

I woke up with a snort, a bit of embarrassing chin drool, and late for work, but —
with one wonderful dream of a plan!

(Even if I do say so myself.)

STEP ONE: Wake-up call.

"Bernice. I need your help tonight with the tooth-taking. Do you mind?"

Bernice yawned. "Huh?"

(Check.)

STEP TWO: Let the tsking begin!

"Tsk. Tsk. Tsk. Edith, this child is untucked!"

"Indeed, Bernice. I see it every night.
Arms poking out from covers here.
Toes sticking out from blankets there."

"Tsk. Tsk."

(Double check.)

STEP THREE : More toes. More tsking.

"Oh dear, oh dear, oh dear. Tsk. Tsk. Tsk."

(Triple check.)

By the time my shift ended, Bernice was extremely perturbed and her tongue very tired from all that tsking.

(My plan could not have been working better.)

"Edith, don't moms and dads do bedtime tucking anymore?"

I dropped my bicuspid bag and rubbed my aching tippy-toe.

"Well, of course they do. But, after all, kids will be kids.

"They wiggle, squirm, they get untucked. Little tootsies get chilled.

"The tots wake up crying.

"Moms and dads lose sleep.

"The Sandman is off schedule.

"And . . . I'm working overtime. It's a most serious problem, all right."

"Yes, I can see that," said Bernice with a knowing nod. "But . . . can't something be done?"

STEP FOUR: A little Edith B. Cuspid magic.
(Not to mention superb acting.)

I sighed a long, long . . . *very long* sigh.

"Yes, if only someone, somewhere
had the answer to this terrible
untucking situation. . . .
But . . . Who? What? How?"

Bernice began thinking . . . thinking . . . thinking.
There was a glint in her twinkle. A flick in her flutter.
The sparkle in Sparklestein was making a comeback!
(Check! Check! Check! Check!)

The very next morning, over a cup of cocoa, Bernice was all aflutter.

"Edith!" she announced with the utmost confidence. "What is needed here, is a Goodnight, Sleeptight, Don't Let the Bed Bugs Bite Fairy Godmother! Someone to make sure children get an extra bedtime tuck."

"What an absolutely incredibly *marvelous* idea! But — Bernice — **Wait!**

". . . That's no job for an ordinary everyday wand waver. Who can we ever get to do it?"

Bernice grinned.

"Edith, my first-class friend — I'm thinking — who you've been thinking. Me."

And, there you have it, my dears.
Like the story always goes . . .
        We all lived happily ever after.

But I bet you knew that already, didn't you?

THE
END!

For my talented sister, Barbara — M.P.

To my mom, Colleen Ajhar, who
never lost her sparkle — B.A.

Text copyright © 2009 by Margie Palatini • Illustrations copyright © 2009 by Brian Ajhar

All rights reserved. Published by Orchard Books, an imprint of Scholastic Inc., *Publishers since 1920*. ORCHARD BOOKS and
design are registered trademarks of Watts Publishing Group, Ltd., used under license. SCHOLASTIC and associated logos are
trademarks and/or registered trademarks of Scholastic Inc. No part of this publication may be reproduced, stored in a retrieval
system, or transmitted in any form or by any means, electronic, mechanical, photocopying, recording, or otherwise, without
written permission of the publisher. For information regarding permission, write to Orchard Books, Scholastic Inc., Permissions
Department, 557 Broadway, New York, NY 10012.

Library of Congress Cataloging-in-Publication Data
Palatini, Margie.
Gone with the wand / Margie Palantini ; illustrations by Brian Ahjar. — 1st ed.
p. cm.
Summary: When tooth fairy Edith B. Cuspid finds her friend Bernice Sparklestein, a fairy godmother whose work
is legendary, having a very bad wand day, she tries to cheer her up by suggesting Bernice try other fairy jobs.
ISBN-13: 978-0-439-72768-6 (reinforced lib. bdg.)
ISBN-10: 0-439-72768-5 (reinforced lib. bdg.)
[1. Fairy godmothers — Fiction. 2. Tooth fairy — Fiction. 3. Fairies — Fiction.
4. Magic — Fiction. 5. Occupations — Fiction.] I. Ahjar, Brian, ill. II. Title.
PZ7.P1755Gnr 2008
[E] — dc22
2007030855

Printed in Singapore   46
Reinforced binding for library use
First edition, April 2009
Book design by Christopher Stengel

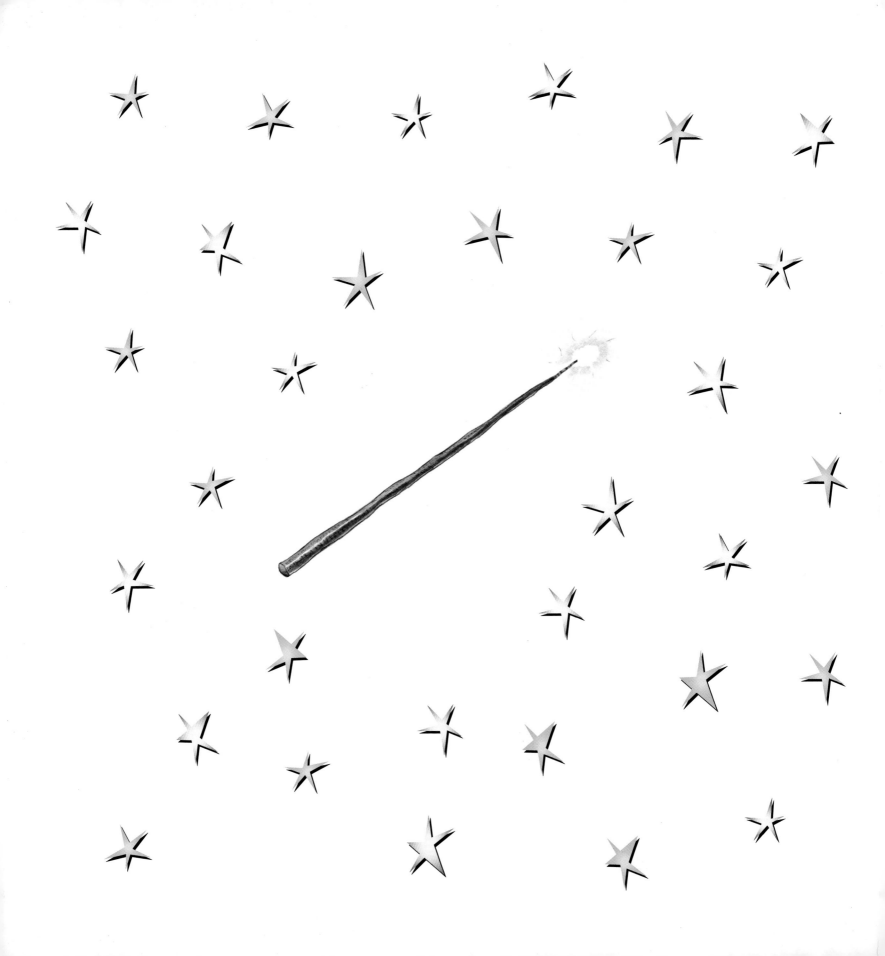